Once Upon a Time in a Faraway Land, a young Prince lived in a shining castle.

KJN002-1

Although he had everything his heart desired, the Prince was spoiled, selfish and unkind.

One winter's night, an old beggar woman came to the castle and offered him a single rose in return for shelter from the bitter cold.

Repulsed by her haggard appearance, the Prince sneered at the gift and turned the old woman away.

But she warned him not to be deceived by appearances ~~ for beauty is found within.

And when he dismissed her again, the old woman's ugliness melted away to reveal...

...a beautiful Enchantress!

The Prince tried to apologize, but it was too late ~~ for she had seen that there was no love in his heart.

As punishment, she transformed the Prince into a hideous Beast...

...and placed a powerful spell on the castle and all who lived there.

Ashamed of his monstrous form, the Beast concealed himself inside his castle with a Magic Mirror as his only window to the outside world.

The rose she had offered was truly an enchanted Rose which would bloom until his 21st year.

If he could learn to love another and earn her love in return by the time the last petal fell, then the spell would be broken.

If not -- he would be doomed to remain a Beast for all time.

As the years passed, he fell into despair and lost all hope...

...for who could ever learn to love a Beast?

And now, 10 years later...

ANOTHER BEAUTIFUL DAY!

ANOTHER TRIP INTO TOWN!

4

NO BEAST ALIVE STANDS A *CHANCE* AGAINST *YOU*, GASTON! HEH HEH--AND NO *GIRL*, FOR THAT MATTER!

--ON *THAT* ONE!

THE *INVENTOR'S* DAUGHTER?

SHE'S THE ONE! THE *LUCKY* GIRL I'M GOING TO MARRY!

IT'S *TRUE*, LEFOU! AND I'VE GOT MY *SIGHTS* SET--

HELLOOOO, BELLE!

BONJOUR, GASTON.

PFOOO!

HOW CAN YOU *READ* THIS? THERE'S NO *PICTURES*!

FWIP!

SOME PEOPLE USE THEIR *IMAGINATIONS*!

BELLE, IT'S ABOUT TIME YOU GOT YOUR *HEAD* OUT OF THESE BOOKS AND PAID ATTENTION TO MORE *IMPORTANT* THINGS--

--LIKE *ME*!

AHHHH!

IT'S NOT RIGHT FOR A *WOMAN* TO READ! SOON SHE STARTS GETTING IDEAS--*THINKING*!

GASTON, YOU ARE POSITIVELY *PRIMEVAL*!

WHY-- *THANK YOU*, BELLE!

NOW WHADDAYA SAY YOU AND I GO LOOK AT MY *TROPHIES*?

UH--MAYBE SOME *OTHER* TIME! I HAVE TO GET HOME AND HELP MY *FATHER*!

THAT CRAZY OLD *LOON* NEEDS ALL THE HELP HE CAN *GET*!

YEAH! HA HA HA!

DON'T TALK ABOUT MY *FATHER* THAT WAY!

5

YEAH! *DON'T* TALK ABOUT HER *FATHER* THAT WAY!

THWAK!

MY FATHER'S NOT *CRAZY*-- --HE'S A *GENIUS!*

KA-BOOM!

PAPA!

PAPA! ⸮coff coff!⸴ PAPA, ARE YOU *ALL RIGHT?* ⸮coff!⸴

HOW ON EARTH DID *THAT* HAPPEN? CAN'T FOR THE *LIFE* OF ME FIGURE OUT...

PAPA!

I'M ABOUT READY TO *GIVE UP* ON THIS HUNK OF *JUNK!*

KLNK!

YOU *ALWAYS* SAY THAT!

I *MEAN* IT THIS TIME! I'LL *NEVER* GET THIS BONE-HEADED *CONTRAPTION* TO WORK!

YES, YOU *WILL!* AND YOU'LL WIN *FIRST PRIZE* AT THE *FAIRE* TOMORROW AND BE A FAMOUS *INVENTOR!*

YOU *REALLY BELIEVE* THAT?

I *ALWAYS HAVE!*

THEN WHAT ARE WE *WAITING* FOR? I'LL HAVE THIS THING FIXED IN *NO* TIME!

PAPA, DO YOU THINK I'M... *ODD*?

MY DAUGHTER? *ODD*? NOW WHERE WOULD YOU GET AN IDEA LIKE *THAT*?

I JUST DON'T FIT IN HERE. I WANT *ADVENTURE*--*EXCITEMENT*-- AND SOMEONE TO *SHARE* IT WITH!

WHAT ABOUT *GASTON*? HE'S A *HANDSOME* FELLA!

NO, THANKS!

WELL, DON'T YOU *WORRY*, 'CAUSE THIS *INVENTION'S* GOING TO BE THE START OF A WHOLE *NEW* LIFE FOR US!

LET'S GIVE HER ANOTHER *TRY*!

CHOONK!

IT *WORKS*, PAPA! YOUR WOOD CHOPPER *WORKS*!

CHOP! CHOP! CHOP!

AND SO...

GOODBYE! *GOOD LUCK*, PAPA!

GOODBYE, BELLE! TAKE *CARE* WHILE I'M *GONE*!

7

HOURS LATER...

WE SHOULD BE *THERE* BY NOW! MAYBE WE MISSED THE *TURN*...

WOLVES!

HA-ROOOOO!

NEEHRHRHR!

HA-ROOOOO!

PHILLIPE-- NOOO--!

SPLOOP!

HA-ROOOOO!

PHILLIPE!

COME BACK!

GRRRR!

HELP! SOMEBODY-- HEEELP!

A GATE!

I'VE GOT TO GET INSIDE!

GRRRR!

INCREDIBLE! HOW IS THIS ACCOMPLISHED? THESE AREN'T *PUPPETS!*

'ALLO, MONSIEUR!

HMM...

SIR! SIR, PUT ME DOWN AT *ONCE* OR I WILL BE FORCED TO GIVE YOU A SOUND *THRASHING!*

WHY... WHY, YOU'RE *ALIVE!*

BUT OF *COURSE!*

AAA-CHOOO!

WHY, YOU ARE *SOAKED* TO THE *BONE*, MONSIEUR!

COME--*WARM* YOURSELF BY THE *FIRE!*

≥sniff!≤ THANK YOU!

NO! LUMIERE, I *FORBID* IT! THE MASTER WILL BE *FURIOUS* IF HE FINDS HIM HERE!

NO NO NO-- NOT THE *MASTER'S* CHAIR!

OH, NO-- NOT THE *DOG!*

SIT! STAY!

ARP! ARP!

WOULD YOU LIKE A SPOT OF *TEA*, SIR? IT'LL WARM YOU UP IN NO TIME!

NO-- NO TEA! *NO TEA!!*

WE'VE GOT TO GET HIM **OUT** OF HERE! YOU **KNOW** WHAT THE MASTER WILL **DO** IF HE--

CALM YOURSELF, COGSWORTH! THE MASTER WILL NEVER HAVE TO **KNOW!**

BUT--

THERE'S A **STRANGER** HERE!

M-MASTER-- ALLOW ME TO **EXPLAIN!**

THE GENTLEMAN WAS **LOST** IN THE WOODS AND--

WHAT ARE **YOU DOING** HERE?

YOU'RE NOT **WELCOME!**

PLEASE-- I MEANT NO HARM-- I JUST NEEDED A PLACE TO STAY!

I'LL GIVE YOU A PLACE TO **STAY!**

MEANWHILE, OUTSIDE BELLE'S COTTAGE...

I'D LIKE TO **THANK** YOU ALL FOR COMING TO MY **WEDDING!**

THIS IS **BELLE'S** LUCKY DAY!

BUT **FIRST**, I'D BETTER GO IN THERE AND **PROPOSE** TO THE GIRL! HA HA!

BOO-HOO!

NOW, LEFOU-- WHEN **BELLE** AND I COME OUT THAT **DOOR**--

I KNOW, I **KNOW**-- STRIKE UP THE BAND!

11

KNOCK KNOCK!

GASTON! WHAT A -- er-- PLEASANT SURPRISE!

ISN'T IT, THOUGH? I'M JUST FULL OF SURPRISES!

THIS IS THE DAY YOUR DREAMS COME TRUE, BELLE!

WHAT DO YOU KNOW ABOUT MY DREAMS, GASTON?

PLENTY!

PICTURE THIS-- A RUSTIC HUNTING LODGE...MY LATEST KILL ROASTING ON THE FIRE...SIX OR SEVEN LITTLE ONES PLAYING ON THE FLOOR WITH THE DOGS... AND MY LITTLE WIFE--

--MASSAGING MY FEET...

DO YOU KNOW WHO THAT LITTLE WIFE WILL BE?

YOU, BELLE!

GASTON-- I REALLY DON'T KNOW WHAT TO SAY!

SAY YOU'LL MARRY ME!

I'M VERY SORRY, GASTON, BUT... BUT...

...BUT THANKS FOR ASKING!

WHOOOA-!!

SHE TURNED YA *DOWN*, HUH?

TURNED *ME* DOWN?! NONSENSE!

SHE'S JUST, UH.... PLAYING *HARD* TO GET!

I'LL HAVE BELLE FOR MY WIFE *ONE* WAY OR *ANOTHER!*

IS HE *GONE?*

BRAAAK!

CAN YOU *IMAGINE?* HE ASKED ME TO *MARRY* HIM! *ME,* THE WIFE OF THAT BOORISH, BRAINLESS--

NEERRHRHR!

PHILLIPE! WHAT ARE *YOU* DOING HERE?

WHERE'S PAPA?!

WHAT *HAPPENED?!* OH, WE HAVE TO *FIND* HIM!

PHILLIPE, YOU HAVE TO *TAKE* ME TO HIM!

AND SOON, DEEP WITHIN THE FOREST...

ALL RIGHT, CALM *DOWN,* PHILLIPE! WHICH WAY DO WE GO NOW?

WHERE *IS* THIS PLACE?

PHILLIPE -- THERE'S PAPA'S *HAT!*

COME ON-- WE'RE GOING INSIDE!

HELLO?

IS ANYONE HERE?

PAPA!

PAPA! IT'S BELLE!

COULDN'T KEEP QUIET, *COULD* WE? JUST HAD TO INVITE HIM TO STAY, *DIDN'T* WE?

I WAS TRYING TO BE *HOSPITABLE!*

HUH??

PAPA!

DID YOU SEE *THAT?* IT'S A *GIRL!*

I KNOW IT'S A GIRL!

WHO -- WHO ARE YOU?

THE MASTER OF THIS CASTLE.

I'VE COME FOR MY FATHER. THERE MUST BE SOME MIS-UNDERSTANDING. PLEASE, LET HIM OUT. CAN'T YOU SEE HE'S SICK?

THEN HE SHOULDN'T HAVE TRESPASSED HERE.

BUT HE COULD DIE! I'LL DO ANYTHING, PLEASE!

THERE MUST BE SOME WAY I CAN CONVINCE YOU--

WAIT! TAKE ME INSTEAD!

YOU WOULD TAKE HIS PLACE?

BELLE, NO--!

IF I STAY, WOULD YOU LET HIM GO?

YES. BUT YOU MUST PROMISE TO STAY HERE FOREVER.

COME INTO THE LIGHT.

YOU HAVE MY WORD.

NO, BELLE! ≳ COFF COFF ≲

NO, I WON'T LET YOU DO THIS--!!

16

TAKE HIM BACK TO THE VILLAGE!

OH, PAPA--!!

WHAT DO I DO? WHAT DO I SAY TO HER?

MASTER?

WHAT?!

UM... SINCE THE GIRL IS GOING TO BE *WITH* US FOR QUITE SOME TIME, I WAS THINKING, ER-- THAT YOU *MIGHT* WANT TO OFFER HER A MORE COMFORTABLE *ROOM!*

GRRR!

THEN AGAIN--MAYBE *NOT!*

YOU DIDN'T EVEN LET ME SAY *GOODBYE!* I'LL NEVER SEE HIM AGAIN!

I'LL SHOW YOU TO YOUR *ROOM.* UNLESS YOU WANT TO STAY IN THE *TOWER,* FOLLOW ME.

SAY SOMETHING TO HER!

I, UH...HOPE YOU'LL *LIKE* IT HERE. THE CASTLE IS YOUR *HOME* NOW, SO YOU CAN GO *ANY-WHERE* YOU LIKE--

--EXCEPT THE *WEST WING.*

WHAT'S IN--?

IT IS FORBIDDEN!

FWISH!

~GROAN~

HERE'S YOUR *ROOM.*

IF YOU *NEED ANYTHING,* MY *SERVANTS* WILL ATTEND YOU.

INVITE HER TO DINNER!

YOU'LL, UH... *JOIN ME FOR DINNER.*

THAT'S *NOT A REQUEST.*

MEANWHILE, AT THE VILLAGE TAVERN...

WHO DOES SHE THINK SHE *IS?* THAT GIRL HAS TANGLED WITH THE *WRONG MAN!*

NO ONE SAYS NO TO GASTON!

DARN *RIGHT!* EH-- MORE *BEER?*

FLUMP!

OH, WHAT FOR? *NOTHING HELPS!* I'M *DISGRACED!* I'VE BEEN PUBLICLY *HUMILIATED!*

IT'S *MORE* THAN I CAN *BEAR...*

GASTON-- YOU'VE GOT TO *PULL* YOURSELF *TOGETHER!* WHY, YOU'RE THE HERO OF THE *TOWN*, THE MAN OF THE *HOUR!*

OH, YEAH, *RIGHT...*

IT JUST *BREAKS* MY HEART TO SEE YOU SO DOWN IN THE DUMPS! *SMILE*, FOR HEAVEN'S SAKE!

THAAAT'S BETTER!

AFTER ALL, GASTON-- YOU'VE GOT A *REPUTATION* TO UPHOLD!

YOU'RE THE ULTIMATE *MANLY MAN*, GASTON! A SYMBOL OF *STRENGTH!* A PINNACLE OF *PROWESS!* A BULWARK OF *BRAWN!*

YOU *LOOK* THE BEST, EH? YOU *HUNT* THE BEST, EH? AND YOU *SPIT* THE BEST! HA HA!

WHY-- YOU'RE *RIGHT*, LEFOU! IT'S AS PLAIN AS THE *GIRLS* AT MY *FEET!*

DARN RIGHT!

LET'S ALL *HEAR* IT FOR *ME!*

HIP HIP-- HOORAY! HIP HIP-- HOORAY! HIP HIP--

HELP! SOMEBODY HELP ME!

MAURICE--? PLEASE, I NEED YOUR HELP! HE'S GOT HER! HE'S GOT HER LOCKED IN A DUNGEON!

WHO?

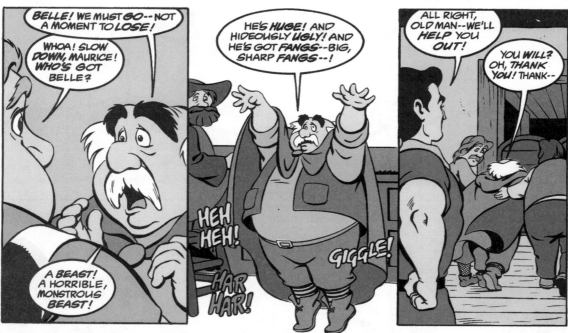

BELLE! WE MUST GO-- NOT A MOMENT TO LOSE!

WHOA! SLOW DOWN, MAURICE! WHO'S GOT BELLE?

HE'S HUGE! AND HIDEOUSLY UGLY! AND HE'S GOT FANGS--BIG, SHARP FANGS--!

ALL RIGHT, OLD MAN--WE'LL HELP YOU OUT!

YOU WILL? OH, THANK YOU! THANK--

A BEAST! A HORRIBLE, MONSTROUS BEAST!

HEH HEH!

HAR HAR!

GIGGLE!

HA HA HA!

CRAZY OL' MAURICE! HE'S ALWAYS GOOD FOR A LAUGH!

--YOOOOOU!

CRAZY OL' MAURICE...

...CRAZY OL' MAURICE. HMMM...

TRY TO BE PATIENT, SIR! THE GIRL HAS LOST HER *FATHER* AND HER *FREEDOM* ALL IN ONE *DAY!*

WHAT'S TAKING HER SO LONG? I TOLD HER TO COME DOWN FOR *DINNER!*

MASTER-- HAVE YOU THOUGHT THAT PERHAPS THIS *GIRL* COULD BE THE ONE TO BREAK THE *SPELL?*

OF *COURSE* I HAVE! I'M *NO FOOL!*

GOOD! SO-- *YOU* FALL IN LOVE WITH *HER* --SHE FALLS IN LOVE WITH *YOU* AND-- *POOF!* THE SPELL IS *BROKEN!*

WE'LL BE *HUMAN* AGAIN BY *MIDNIGHT!*

IT'S NOT THAT *EASY*, LUMIERE! THESE THINGS TAKE *TIME!*

BUT THE *ROSE* HAS ALREADY BEGUN TO *WILT!*

IT'S NO USE. SHE'S SO *BEAUTIFUL*, AND I'M ...

...WELL, LOOK AT ME!

YOU MUST HELP HER SEE PAST ALL THAT!

I DON'T KNOW *HOW!*

IMPRESS HER WITH YOUR RAPIER *WIT!*

BUT BE *GENTLE!*

SHOWER HER WITH COMPLIMENTS!

BUT BE *SINCERE!*

AND ABOVE ALL--

--YOU *MUST* CONTROL YOUR *TEMPER!*

WAIT-- HERE SHE IS!

KA-CHK!

WELL--WHERE *IS* SHE?

WHO? OH, HA HA -- THE *GIRL!* YES, UM...WELL, *ACTUALLY,* UH ... SHE'S IN THE *PROCESS* OF...

...WELL, CIRCUMSTANCES BEING WHAT THEY *ARE*...

...SHE'S NOT COMING!

YOUR *LORDSHIP!* YOUR *GRACE!* YOUR *EMINENCE!*

LET'S NOT BE HASTY!

I *THOUGHT* I TOLD YOU TO COME DOWN TO *DINNER!*

I'M *NOT* HUNGRY!

RAP RAP RAP!

YOU COME OUT OR I'LL *BREAK DOWN* THE *DOOR!*

MASTER, I COULD BE *WRONG* BUT--THAT MAY *NOT* BE THE BEST WAY TO WIN THE GIRL'S AFFECTIONS!

GENTLY-- GENTLY!

GRRRR....OH.... *HMPH!*

IT WOULD GIVE ME GREAT *PLEASURE* IF YOU WOULD JOIN ME FOR *DINNER*...UH, PLEASE!

NO, THANK YOU.

YOU *CAN'T* STAY IN THERE *FOREVER!*

YES, I *CAN!*

FINE! THEN *GO* AHEAD AND *STARVE!*

IF SHE DOESN'T EAT WITH *ME*, SHE DOESN'T EAT AT *ALL!*

OH, *DEAR!*

WE *MIGHT* AS WELL GO *DOWNSTAIRS* AND *CLEAN UP!*

I ASK *NICELY*, BUT SHE *REFUSES!* I'M DOING THE BEST I *CAN!*

WHAT DOES SHE WANT ME TO DO-- *BEG??*

THWUMP!

THWOMP!

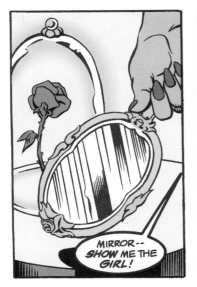

MIRROR-- *SHOW* ME THE GIRL!

THE MASTER'S NOT SO *BAD* ONCE YOU GET TO *KNOW* HIM. WHY DON'T YOU GIVE HIM A *CHANCE?*

I DON'T *WANT* TO GET TO *KNOW* HIM! I DON'T WANT ANYTHING TO *DO* WITH HIM!

SIGH I'M JUST *FOOLING* MYSELF. SHE'LL *NEVER* SEE ME AS ANYTHING BUT A *MONSTER.*

IT'S *HOPELESS*...

COME **ON**, CHIP-- INTO THE **CUPBOARD** WITH YOUR **BROTHERS** AND **SISTERS**!

BUT I'M NOT **SLEEPY**, MAMA!

YES, YOU **ARE**!

HELLO?

AH, **SPLENDID** TO SEE YOU OUT AND ABOUT, MADEMOISELLE!

I AM **COGSWORTH**, HEAD OF THE **HOUSEHOLD**!

ZUT ALORS! SHE HAS **EMERGED**!

I'D **BETTER** TELL COGSWORTH!

AND THIS IS **LUMIERE**...

ENCHANTÉE, CHERIE!

ZIP!

HOW MAY WE **HELP** YOU?

WELL-- I AM A LITTLE **HUNGRY**!

HEAR THAT? SHE'S **HUNGRY**!

STOKE THE **FIRE**-- BREAK OUT THE **SILVER**-- WAKE THE **CHINA**--!

NOW **WAIT**-- REMEMBER WHAT THE **MASTER** SAID!

OH, PISH-TOSH! I'M **NOT** ABOUT TO LET THE POOR CHILD GO HUNGRY!

YOU ARE OUR HONORED GUEST, MADEMOISELLE! LET US PULL UP A CHAIR FOR YOU! RELAX AS THE DINING ROOM PROUDLY PRESENTS--

--YOUR DINNER!

TAKE A GLANCE AT THE MENU, CHÉRIE -- SOUP DU JOUR! HOT HORS D'OEUVRES!

WE LIVE ONLY TO SERVE, AND WE SERVE ONLY THE BEST!

YOU'RE ALONE HERE, AND AFRAID, BUT LOOK-- THE BANQUET IS PREPARED! EVERY DISH IN PERFECT TASTE AND SERVED WITH FLAIR!

AFTER ALL, MISS, THIS IS FRANCE--ALL THE DISHES SING AND DANCE! LET US SERVE YOU A CULINARY CABARET!

THERE'S BEEF RAGOUT AND CHEESE SOUFFLE! AND TRY THE PIE AND PUDDING--

--EN FLAMBÉ!

FWOOF!

YOU'RE A GUEST--A REAL GUEST! THANK HEAVENS I'VE HAD THE NAPKINS FRESHLY PRESSED!

YOU'LL WANT TEA WITH DESSERT, SO I MUST BREW THE WATER NICE AND HOT!

25

IT'S BEEN SO LONG SINCE WE'VE HAD A SOUL TO *WAIT* UPON-- TEN WHOLE YEARS WE'VE BEEN RUSTING!

THEN IN YOU WALK AND UPS-A-DAISY!

YOUR REQUEST IS OUR *COMMAND!* LET US *SERVE* AND *ENTERTAIN* YOU!

OUR ONLY AIM IS TO *PLEASE* YOU--

--OUR *GUEST!*

WOULD YOU LIKE A *TOUR,* MADEMOISELLE?

OH, YES!

WAIT! WAIT A SECOND! I'M NOT SURE THAT'S A *GOOD* IDEA, LUMIERE!

PERHAPS *YOU'D* LIKE TO *TAKE* ME! I'M SURE *YOU* KNOW *EVERYTHING* THERE IS TO KNOW ABOUT THE CASTLE!

WELL, ACTUALLY... I *DO!*

AND SO, MANY ROOMS AND CORRIDORS LATER...

NOW THEN-- IF I MAY DRAW YOUR ATTENTION TO THE *FLYING BUTTRESSES*--

THE *WEST WING*...

WAIT! DON'T GO!

PLEASE-- MADEMOISELLE!

SOON...

WE MADE IT, PHILLIPE! NOW WE JUST HAVE TO *FIND* OUR WAY *HOME!*

HA-OOOOOO!

OH, NO...

GRRRRR!

RUN, PHILLIPE-- *RUN!*

FASTER, PHILLIPE--

--RUN FASTER!!

GRRRR!

GRRRR! REERHRHR!!

YIIEEE!

LATER, AT THE BEAST'S CASTLE...

HERE, NOW-- DON'T *DO* THAT!

JUST HOLD STILL AND LET ME--

ROAAAR!

GASP!

THAT HURTS!!

IF YOU'D HOLD *STILL,* IT WOULDN'T HURT AS MUCH!

IF YOU HADN'T RUN *AWAY,* THIS WOULDN'T HAVE *HAPPENED!*

IF YOU HADN'T *FRIGHTENED* ME, I WOULDN'T HAVE RUN AWAY!

WELL, YOU SHOULDN'T HAVE BEEN IN THE *WEST WING.*

AND *YOU* SHOULD LEARN TO CONTROL YOUR *TEMPER!*

NOW HOLD *STILL*-- THIS MAY *STING* A LITTLE!

NNNNG--!

BY THE WAY...

...*THANK YOU* FOR SAVING MY *LIFE.*

≑whew!≑

LATE THAT NIGHT, IN THE VILLAGE TAVERN...

THANK YOU FOR COMING ON SUCH SHORT *NOTICE,* MONSIEUR D'ARQUE!

MAISON de LOONES

I DON'T *USUALLY* LEAVE THE ASYLUM IN THE MIDDLE OF THE *NIGHT,* BUT HE SAID YOU'D MAKE IT WORTH MY *WHILE!*

THAT I *DID!*

CLINK!

IT'S LIKE THIS-- I'VE GOT MY *HEART* SET ON MARRYING *BELLE,* BUT SHE NEEDS A LITTLE...*PERSUASION!*

TURNED HIM DOWN *FLAT!*

EVERYONE KNOWS HER FATHER'S A *LUNATIC!* HE WAS IN HERE TONIGHT RAVING ABOUT A *BEAST* IN A *CASTLE!*

THWAK!

AH! YOU WANT ME TO THROW HER *FATHER* INTO THE *ASYLUM* UNTIL SHE AGREES TO MARRY YOU!

OH, THAT'S *DESPICABLE!*

I *LOVE* IT!

31

WHILE AT BELLE'S COTTAGE...

IF NO ONE WILL *HELP* ME, THEN I'LL GO BACK *ALONE!*

LET'S SEE... MY *COMPASS*... OH, AND MY *MAPS*...

I DON'T *CARE* WHAT IT *TAKES* -- I'LL *FIND* THAT CASTLE AND SOMEHOW--

--I'LL GET BELLE *OUT* OF THERE!

AND ONLY MOMENTS LATER...

BELLE? MAURICE?

I'M *AFRAID* THERE'S NO ONE *HOME!*

THEY HAVE TO COME BACK *SOMETIME!* AND WHEN THEY *DO*--

--WE'LL BE *READY* FOR THEM!

AND THE NEXT MORNING...

I'VE NEVER *FELT* THIS WAY ABOUT ANYONE! I WANT TO DO SOMETHING FOR HER...

...BUT *WHAT?*

FLOWERS? CHOCOLATES?

NO NO--THIS IS NO ORDINARY GIRL! IT HAS TO BE SOMETHING VERY *SPECIAL*... SOMETHING THAT SPARKS HER *INTEREST!*

A-HAA-- I KNOW *JUST* THE THING!

AND SO TIME PASSES...

BUT WHO WOULD HAVE THOUGHT...

...WHO COULD HAVE GUESSED...

...WHAT MIGHT HAPPEN IN THAT TIME?

LATER...

TONIGHT IS THE NIGHT!

I'M NOT SURE I CAN DO THIS...

MASTER, YOU DON'T HAVE TIME TO BE TIMID! YOU CARE FOR THE GIRL, DON'T YOU?

MORE THAN ANYTHING!

WELL THEN -- YOU MUST TELL HER! YOU CAN DO IT!

I CAN DO IT!

THAT EVENING, THEY DANCE...

...AND AFTERWARDS...

BELLE, ARE YOU *HAPPY* HERE... WITH *ME?*

YES.

WHAT'S THE *MATTER?*

IF ONLY I COULD SEE MY *FATHER* AGAIN... JUST FOR A MOMENT. I *MISS* HIM SO MUCH.

THERE IS A *WAY.*

THAT MIRROR WILL SHOW YOU *ANYTHING* YOU WISH TO *SEE.*

I'D LIKE TO SEE MY *FATHER,* PLEASE.

WHAT DID YOU *SAY?*

I *RELEASE* YOU. YOU'RE NO LONGER MY *PRISONER.*

I'M--I'M *FREE?*

YES.

BELLE! ⸘coff coff‽ BELLE--!

PAPA!

OH, HE'S *SICK*-- HE MAY BE *DYING!* AND HE'S ALL *ALONE!*

THEN... YOU MUST GO TO HIM.

TAKE THE MIRROR WITH YOU. SO YOU'LL ALWAYS HAVE A WAY TO LOOK BACK... AND *REMEMBER* ME.

THANK YOU FOR UNDERSTANDING!

WELL, YOUR HIGHNESS -- I MUST SAY, EVERYTHING IS GOING *SWIMMINGLY!* I KNEW YOU HAD IT IN YOU!

I LET HER GO.

WHAT??? HOW COULD YOU DO THAT?!

I HAD TO.

WHY?!

BECAUSE I LOVE HER.

HE WHAT?

YES, I'M AFRAID IT'S *TRUE.*

SHE'S GOING AWAY?

BUT HE WAS SO *CLOSE!*

PHILLIPE, WE'VE GOT TO *FIND* HIM! THE MIRROR SAYS HE'S *THIS* WAY! HURRY!

PAPA!!

RUN, BELLE... *RUN!* IT SHOULD HAVE BEEN *ME...*

SOON, BACK AT THE COTTAGE...

IT SHOULD HAVE BEEN *ME...* ME...

IT'S ALL RIGHT, PAPA-- I'M *HOME!*

B-BELLE? BELLE!

YOU REALLY *HAVE* COME HOME! I THOUGHT I'D NEVER *SEE* YOU AGAIN!

BUT THE *BEAST*-- HOW DID YOU *ESCAPE?*

I *DIDN'T* ESCAPE--HE LET ME *GO!*

HE'S *DIFFERENT* NOW, PAPA! HE'S *CHANGED* SOMEHOW!

OH! A STOWAWAY!

HI!

BONK!

THUNK!

37

WHY, *HELLO* THERE, LITTLE FELLA! I DIDN'T THINK I'D LIKE TO SEE *YOU* AGAIN!

BELLE, WHY'D YOU GO *AWAY?* DON'T YOU *LIKE US* ANYMORE?

KNOCK KNOCK!

MAY I *HELP* YOU?

I'VE COME TO COLLECT YOUR *FATHER!*

MY *FATHER--?*

DON'T *WORRY,* MADEMOISELLE! WE'LL TAKE *GOOD CARE* OF HIM!

MY FATHER'S NOT *CRAZY!*

OH? HEY, MAURICE! TELL US *AGAIN,* OLD MAN-- JUST HOW BIG *WAS* THAT BEAST?

WELL, HE, UH, HE WAS *ENORMOUS!* I'D SAY *EIGHT--* NO, MORE LIKE *TEN* FEET TALL!

HA HA HA! FOLKS, YOU DON'T GET MUCH CRAZIER THAN *THAT!*

POOR BELLE! IT'S A *SHAME* ABOUT YOUR FATHER!

YOU *KNOW* HE'S NOT CRAZY, GASTON!

HMM! I MAY BE ABLE TO CLEAR UP THIS LITTLE MISUNDERSTANDING IF--

--YOU MARRY ME!

ONE LITTLE *WORD*, BELLE! THAT'S ALL IT TAKES!

NEVER!

HAVE IT *YOUR WAY*, THEN!

WAIT! MY FATHER'S *NOT* CRAZY, AND I CAN *PROVE* IT!

MIRROR-- *SHOW* ME THE BEAST!

FLASH!

SEE? THERE HE *IS!* MY FATHER WAS TELLING THE *TRUTH!*

IS HE *DANGEROUS?*

OH, NO--HE'D NEVER HURT ANYONE! I KNOW HE LOOKS VICIOUS, BUT HE'S REALLY KIND AND GENTLE!

HE'S... HE'S MY FRIEND!

IF I DIDN'T KNOW BETTER, I'D THINK YOU HAVE FEELINGS FOR THIS MONSTER!

HE'S NO MONSTER, GASTON!

YOU ARE!

SHE'S AS CRAZY AS THE OLD MAN!

GASTON--!!

THE BEAST WILL MAKE OFF WITH YOUR CHILDREN! HE'LL COME AFTER THEM IN THE NIGHT!

WE'RE NOT SAFE UNTIL HIS HEAD IS MOUNTED ON MY WALL! I SAY--

--KILL THE BEAST!

KILL THE BEAST!

I WON'T LET YOU *DO* THIS!

IF YOU'RE NOT *WITH* US, YOU'RE *AGAINST* US!

BRING THE *OLD MAN!* LET'S LOCK THEM UP! WE CAN'T HAVE THEM RUNNING OFF TO *WARN* THE CREATURE!

GET YOUR HANDS OFF ME!

IN YOU GO, LOONY!

YOU'RE *NEXT,* BELLE!

NOOOO--!

SLAM!

LET US OUT!

THUMP! THUMP!

I HAVE TO WARN THE *BEAST!* THIS IS ALL MY FAULT! OH, PAPA, WHAT ARE WE GOING TO DO?!

NOW, NOW-- WE'LL THINK OF *SOMETHING!*

SOON, AT THE BEAST'S CASTLE ...

SACRE BLEU-- INVADERS!

AND THEY HAVE THE MIRROR!

WE'VE GOT TO WARN THE MASTER!

TAKE WHATEVER BOOTY YOU CAN FIND, BUT REMEMBER--THE BEAST IS MINE!

KILL THE BEAST!

BOOM!

KILL THE BEAST!

BOOM!

PARDON ME, MASTER--?

LEAVE ME IN PEACE.

BUT, SIR-- THE CASTLE IS UNDER ATTACK!

NOOOO!

...BELLE?!

ROARRR!

ROARRR!

AHHK--!!

LET ME GO-- ≳choke!≲ -- LET ME GO!

PLEASE, DON'T HURT ME! I'LL DO ANYTHING--!